For all those who work for peace in the world,
and for all those who don't.

SALMAGUNDI

First published 1985

ISBN 0 19 558117 2

Typeset by Whitcoulls Ltd, Christchurch, New Zealand
Printed by Hip Shing Printers Ltd, Hong Kong
Published by Oxford University Press,
5 Ramsgate Street, Auckland 5, New Zealand

SALMAGUNDI

written by
JOY COWLEY

illustrated by
PHILIP WEBB

Oxford University Press Auckland Melbourne Oxford

Once there was a town called Garpen Flat. Its name was on the map, and also on the railway station. But no one could see the town itself because it was covered with a thick brown smog.

The smog came from two factories, one on the north side, one to the south. All day these factories clonged and clanged and spat smoke from their chimneys. Smoke hid the shops and houses. Smoke lay over the roads. Smoke covered everything like a huge brown blanket.

The people in Garpen Flat never saw the sun. Their eyes were always red. Their faces were as pale as peeled potatoes. They coughed on their way to work in the factories, and they coughed on their way home again.

The children of the town were as pale as little mushrooms. They had no parks to play in, no trees to climb, for nothing would grow in the smog. No bird ever sang in the streets. All that could be heard was the clonging and the clanging and the coughing.

The factory on the north side was owned by a woman called Doctor Foster. She made missiles to blow up tanks. The factory on the south side was owned by a man called Major Brassblow. He made tanks to shoot down missiles. The missiles and the tanks were sold to far-off countries which were having wars.

Because the Doctor and the Major made lots of money from their factories, they didn't have to live in the smog. They each had a grand house high in the hills, where the air was always clean. They had large gardens and orchards where birds sang. They had secretaries and servants and swimming pools. Doctor Foster's kitchen was covered with peacock feathers. Major Brassblow ate liquorice allsorts from a dish made of carved moon rock. They were both greatly rich. They were also greatly alike, which is why they were enemies. When one thought of something, the other very often thought of it too.

MAJOR BRASSBLOW
MAJOR BRASSBLOW
PRIVATE
KEEP

One morning, Doctor Foster called her secretary. 'Tim, Tim, come here! That diabolical Major Brassblow is plotting some deadly deed. Look at my hair! It has got a curl in it. My hair only goes curly when he's up to some trickery.'

'It looks very nice curly,' said Tim who was always polite.

Doctor Foster scowled into her mirror. 'I'd love to know what he's planning. Is he going to make stouter and stronger tanks to shoot down missiles? I intend to find out.'

'How, Doctor?' asked Tim.

'By salmagundi!' hissed the Doctor.

'Salmagundi?' said Tim. 'That's a kind of salad.'

'It's too good a word for salad,' she replied. 'I'm going to use it for spying. I'll disguise myself as a poor old woman. Then I'll be off to do some salmagundi in the Brassblow Tank Factory.'

'Isn't that rather dangerous?' said Tim.

'Who cares about danger?' cried Doctor Foster. 'Bring me some tattered clothes. Find me a rattly-bang old car. If anyone phones, tell them I've gone to a peace conference in London.'

'Are you sure you're doing the right thing?' Tim asked timidly.

'Right? Right?' Doctor Foster gave a nasty laugh. 'I tell you, Tim, salmagundi is the only way.'

On the hill in the distance, Major Brassblow was having breakfast. He was eating a boiled egg in a gold and ruby eggcup, when suddenly his toes began to twitch. 'Aha!' he said. 'Something is afoot!' He got up from the table and called his secretary. 'Jane, Jane, my toes are twitching!'

Jane came running. She knew all about the Major's toes. 'What's that fiendish Doctor Foster doing now?' she cried.

'I don't know,' growled the Major. 'But when my toes twitch this bad, I can be sure she's up to no good. Who can tell? Perhaps she's building bigger and better missiles to blow up tanks. I must find out.'

'What will you do?' asked Jane.

'I don't know,' he growled again. Then he said, 'Wait a minute. A word has just popped into my head. Salmagundi!'

'It means salad,' said Jane.

'No, it doesn't. I think it means – spying. Yes, yes, that's it. What a good idea. I'll spy on her missile factory.'

'She'll catch you,' Jane warned.

'Not if I disguise myself,' he said. 'Get me the clothes of an old beggar, and a rattly-bang truck. Don't tell anyone where I've gone.'

'What if someone calls?' said Jane.

'Say that I've gone to the disarmament talks in Washington,' he replied.

Major Brassblow put on old clothes, got in the rattly-bang truck and went down into the town, down into the thick brown smog. At the same time, Doctor Foster put on old clothes, got in a rattly-bang car and went down into the town, down into the thick brown smog.

Neither of them could see where they were going. The Doctor went up the street in the car, as the Major came down it in the truck. They met in the middle with a rattle and a bang. The car and the truck, being old, promptly fell to bits.

Doctor Foster got out of the wreck in a great fury. She stumbled through the smog, bellowing, 'Look at my car, you fool!'

Major Brassblow stamped towards her. 'Idiot of a driver!' he shouted. 'You shouldn't be on the road.'

They got close enough to recognize each other. There was a stunned silence.

'It's *you*!' cried the Doctor.

'*You*!' yelled Major Brassblow.

For another moment they stared at each other, then they began to hop up and down with rage.

'Caught you!' roared Major Brassblow. 'Just in time to foil your foul and fiendish plot.'

'I've caught you, you mean!' shrieked the Doctor. 'Don't pretend you're innocent. I know your deadly diabolical deeds.'

They stood in the middle of the road, calling each other names.

Doctor Foster put her face close to Major Brassblow's. 'Do you know what salmagundi means?'

'Spying!' the Major replied.

'Not now, it doesn't,' cried Doctor Foster. 'Now it means fighting!' And she punched him fair and square on the nose.

'I promised I'd never hit a woman,' yelped Major Brassblow. 'But for you, I'd break any promise.' Then he punched her on the nose.

A furious fight broke out with kicking and punching, biting and scratching, shoving and slapping, and names that are best not remembered. They might have been badly hurt, had not a policeman come along.

'Enough of that!' said the policeman, pulling them apart. 'You two ought to be ashamed of yourselves. I've a good mind to arrest you and throw you in the clink.'

'I beg your pardon!' snapped Major Brassblow, wiping his bleeding nose. 'My good man, do you know who I am? I'm Major Brassblow of the Brassblow Tank Factory. I own half of this town.'

'That's right,' said the Doctor. 'I'm Doctor Foster, and I own the other half.'

The policeman laughed. 'Well, well. I'm Donald Duck and I hate to see husband and wife fighting.'

The Major and the Doctor stared at him.

'Husband and wife?' roared the Major.

'Wife and husband?' screamed the Doctor.

It was a moment before the hugeness of the insult sank in. Then they both turned and attacked the policeman.

The fight didn't last for long. The policeman blew his whistle. Others came to help. Soon the wretched pair were handcuffed and in a van on the way to the police station. There they were put in a small dark cell.

'Let me out!' yelled the Major. 'I am Major Brassblow!'

Doctor Foster rattled the bars. 'I'm Doctor Foster, and you men are going to pay for this!'

But as time passed, their tempers cooled. They were hungry. They had only bread to eat and water to drink. They were cold and there was only one blanket. Being unable to share it, they tore it in half.

'All this is your fault,' complained the Major.

'Trust you to blame someone else,' muttered the Doctor.

And so they spent the night, complaining and muttering and shivering on either side of the dark cell.

In the morning, they were taken to the court house and stood before the Judge.

The Judge put on his spectacles. 'Hmm. Who are these two miserable wrecks?'

The policeman smiled. 'The only names they'll give, your honour, are Doctor Foster and Major Brassblow.'

'That's true!' shouted the Major and the Doctor together.

'Giving the wrong name is a serious charge,' frowned the Judge.

'I tell you, my name is Brassblow,' snapped the Major.

'And I'm Doctor Foster,' said the Doctor.

The Judge turned to the policeman. 'Did they have anything on them to say who they were?'

'Nothing, your honour,' said the policeman. 'Their pockets were empty.'

'That's because these are not my clothes!' said the Major.

'Nor mine!' the Doctor added.

'Stolen clothing!' said the Judge. Then he asked the policeman, 'What about the car and the truck? Did you find their driver's licenses?'

'No, your honour. Nothing there either.'

'My driver's license is in my own car, you fool!' cried Doctor Foster to the policeman.

'So is mine!' said the Major.

'Stolen vehicles,' said the Judge, writing in his book.

'Don't be ridiculous!' the Major said. 'All you have to do is phone my secretary –'

'You'll soon find out who we really are,' said the Doctor, 'and then you'll be sorry.'

The policeman smiled again and said to the Judge, 'Your honour, I checked just to make sure. Doctor Foster is at a peace conference in London. Major Brassblow is attending the disarmament talks in Washington. They're both out of the country, your honour.'

'That's not true!' shouted the Major and the Doctor.

'Silence!' roared the Judge. 'I'll tell you what's true and not true. Look at this list of charges – careless driving, causing an accident, fighting in the street, assaulting a policeman, false information, impersonating famous people, stolen clothes, stolen vehicles, shouting in court, and bad manners. I've never seen so much salmagundi in all my life.' He looked at them over his spectacles. 'Do you know what salmagundi means?'

'Salad!' they said together.

'That's what you say,' said the Judge. 'But I say it means wickedness. And you two are as full of wickedness as anyone I've met. But I know how to fix it. You!' He pointed to the Doctor. 'You are sentenced to six months of hard labour in the tanks factory. And you!' He glared at the Major. 'You can spend six months building missiles. I assure you, those two factories can cure the worst cases of salmagundi. Off you go!'

The Major and the Doctor were dragged away. They yelled. They raged. They wept. They pleaded. But no one would listen to another word they said. The Major was taken to a prison at the north end of town, near Doctor Foster's Missile Factory. The Doctor went in the opposite direction, to a prison near Major Brassblow's Tank Factory.

And so began the most miserable days of their lives.

At six o'clock every morning, the Major was given a piece of bread for breakfast. Then he was taken to the missile factory and chained to a place in the assembly line. At seven o'clock the factory started up. The machines roared, the walls shuddered, and brown smoke came out of the chimneys. The air was filled with a clong, clonging noise.

For twelve hours Major Brassblow had to work in one place, tightening nuts on missiles as they came past. He tightened thirty nuts a minute, and was given half an hour off for lunch. By the time the factory stopped at seven o'clock at night, he had tightened twenty thousand and seven hundred nuts. He was then marched through the smog to the prison where he was given bread for his tea.

Each night in his dreams, Major Brassblow tightened another twenty thousand and seven hundred nuts.

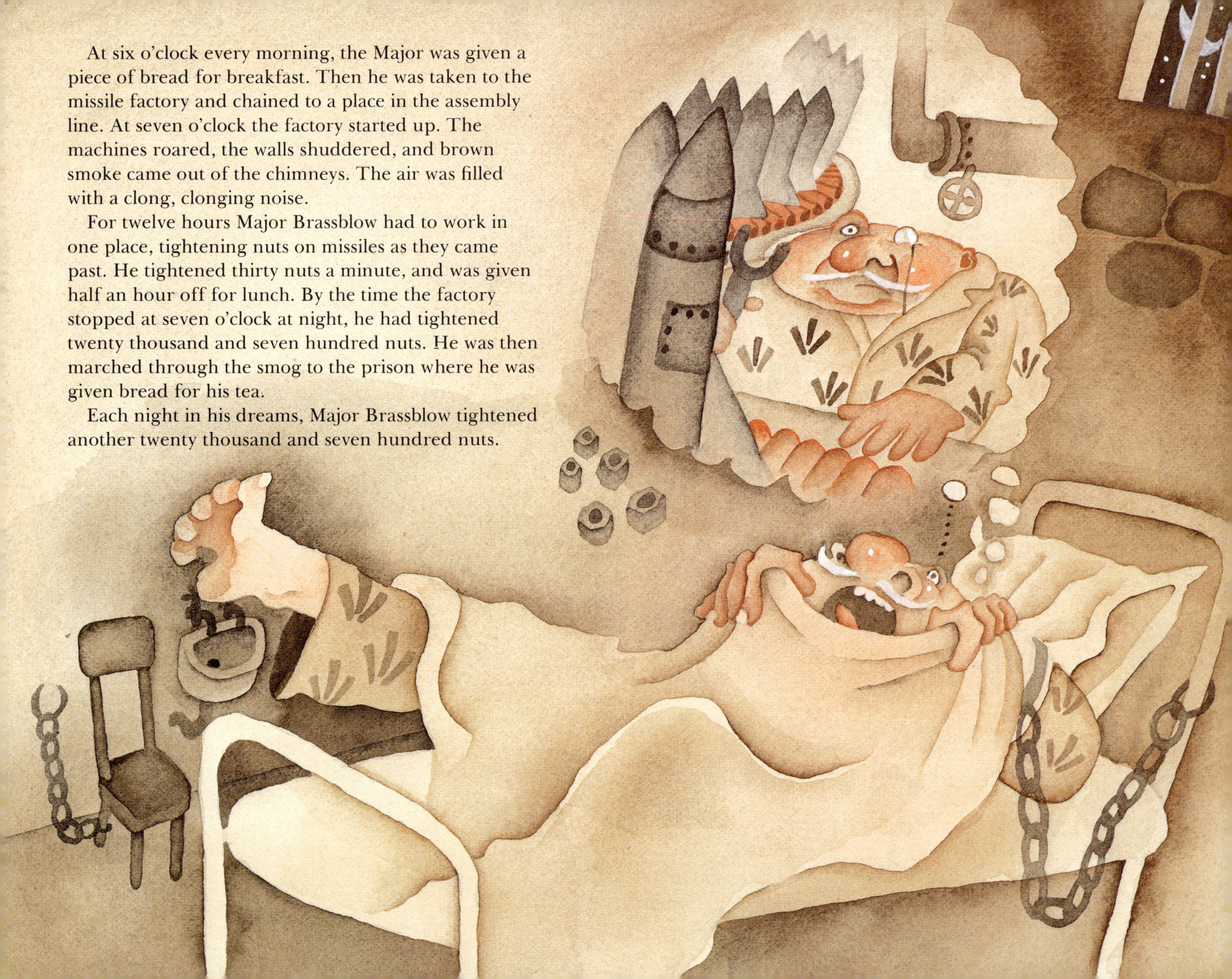

Doctor Foster started her day in much the same way. She was marched to the Brassblow Tank Factory and there she too was chained to a place in the assembly line. At seven o'clock the machinery started up with a clang, clanging noise and brown smoke poured out of the chimneys. Doctor Foster was in charge of an arc welder. As the big tanks rolled past, she had to weld their steel plates. At twenty plates a minute, she welded thirteen thousand and eight hundred a day. At night, in her prison cell, all she could see was the flashes and smoke from the arc welder. And all she could hear was its blowfly buzz.

Hundreds of people worked in the tank factory. The noise was so loud, no one could talk except in the lunch break. The people went out for their lunch, but because she was chained and couldn't move far, the Doctor had to stay in the factory and eat by herself.

One day, the man next to Doctor Foster, sat with her to keep her company. He even offered to share his lunch with her.

'Bread!' sniffed Doctor Foster. 'Haven't you got anything else?'

'What's wrong with bread?' laughed the man.

'Don't you have an apple?'

'Can't grow apples in Garpen Flat,' said the man. 'Too much smog.'

The Doctor looked at him. 'You don't have to work here. Why do you stay in this horrible place?'

'It's all right,' he said.

'All right? It's diabolical! You'd be much better off working in that missile factory.'

'I've tried there,' he said, 'and they're both the same. There's no other work in town. Never mind, Lady. When you get tired, just think of all the good you're doing.'

'What do you mean – good?' said the Doctor.

'Well,' said the man, 'if we didn't make tanks for other countries, they wouldn't win any wars, would they? It'd be a pretty poor show if we couldn't help our far-off friends.'

'Who told you such rubbish?' said the Doctor.

'It isn't rubbish,' said the man. 'Don't you ever read the newspapers? Don't you watch TV? Major Brassblow – he's explained it all.'

The Doctor dropped her bread, and she stamped on it in rage. 'That vile and viperous villain!'

'Hold on,' said the man. 'Don't you go saying things like that. Major Brassblow is a great man. If it weren't for him, the bad people would rule the world. You should be very thankful to Major Brassblow – him and that brilliant Doctor Foster.'

Doctor Foster smiled. 'Come here,' she said. 'No. Closer. Listen. What would you say if I told you I was Doctor Foster?'

The man laughed and laughed. 'I'd say you were nuts.'

After a week in the missile factory, Major Brassblow thought he would die. His toes hardly twitched at all. But his right hand twitched so badly from tightening nuts, that he couldn't hold his bread still to get it into his mouth.

'I can't eat my lunch,' he moaned to the woman in charge of the assembly line.

'Hold it in the other hand then,' she said. She sniffed. 'You prisoners are all the same. All you do is complain. You forget that we have to work just as hard as you.'

'I don't know how you stand it,' said the Major. 'Why don't you get out of here. Go and work in my – in the tank factory. It's a far better place.'

'You have to be joking,' said the woman. 'It's no different from this except it clangs instead of clongs. Never mind, matie. Look on the bright side. Think of what you're doing for the world.'

The Major sighed. 'What are we doing for the world?'

'Listen,' said the woman. 'You got to have peace. Right? And you can't have peace while countries are still at war. And a war's not going to finish until someone wins. Right? And no one's going to win unless we give them weapons. In this factory we are making missiles for world peace. Isn't that terrific?'

'Where did you hear such piffle?' said the Major.

'You prisoners are an ignorant lot! Haven't you ever heard of the famous scientist Doctor Foster?'

The Major choked on his bread. 'That foul and fiendish spy!'

The woman grabbed him by the shoulders. 'You watch it, matie. One word against Doctor Foster, and I'll tell the Judge on you. Right now that wonderful Doctor Foster and that magnificent Major Brassblow are overseas, working for peace for the world. She shook him. 'Aren't you grateful to them?'

Major Brassblow shut his eyes in despair. 'I'd give anything for a bit of peace,' he whispered.

For the first two weeks in the factory, Major Brassblow was so tired, he didn't have a plot or a plan in him. He lost his healthy sun tan. His skin became as pale as a peeled potato and his eyes grew red from the smog. He wondered why his secretary Jane didn't come and rescue him. He felt very sorry for himself.

At the beginning of the third week, his strength began to come back, and with it, his wicked cunning. All at once, he realized the importance of his position.

Here I am, he thought, right in the middle of Doctor Foster's missile factory. That's interesting. I am surrounded by explosives. Very interesting. I have lunch on my own. Ah ha! Very very interesting. Now, if I could make a time bomb and put it under the assembly belt . . .

The Major laughed a devilish laugh and rubbed his hands together. He hadn't felt so happy in days – weeks – years, in fact. What a marvellously simple plan!

What he forgot, however, was that he and the Doctor were very alike in wickedness, and they caught each other's ideas like cold germs.

Doctor Foster woke up in her prison cell. She didn't need a mirror to tell her that her hair was curly. But that didn't worry her. She was too busy thinking about a wonderful plan she had. *Bomb*! she had thought suddenly. I can make a bomb and blow up the tank factory. That'll put an end to all those rivets and it'll fix the mouldy old Major for good. Oh, what a clever scientist I am! I'll put a timing device on the bomb so it goes off at night when the factory is empty. What an explosion! What brilliance!

She was laughing so much, she couldn't eat her breakfast bread.

That day, during the lunch break, she stole some tank ammunition and hid it down the neck of her prison overalls. She put some wire in one pocket, an old clock in another, some pliers in a third. She tucked bits and pieces down her left boot, and odds and ends in her right. After work, she laughed all the way through the smog to her cell. Then, in the small hours of the morning, when everyone was asleep, she made a fiendish time bomb. She was so excited that she didn't notice her hair go from curly to frizzy.

The next day she carried the bomb to work down the front of her overalls. She waited until the lunch break when the factory was quiet and she was on her own. Then she put the bomb, set for midnight, under the assembly belt. Its quiet tick-tock tick-tock was soon buried under the clanging of the machinery.

'A marvellous plan!' laughed the Doctor, welding plates on tanks at double speed. 'I'm so clever, I get dazzled by my own brilliance!'

After tea, Doctor Foster sat up in her prison bed, wide awake. She hadn't been this excited since she was a child and had set a trap in the fireplace for Father Christmas. Five minutes to twelve. Four minutes. Three, two, one minute. Right on midnight it happened, just as she'd planned. First there was the small explosion of her bomb. Then there was a huge sky-splitting, earth-shaking explosion as all the ammunition in the tank factory blew up.

Outside the prison, the night was brighter than day. A fierce orange light filled the Doctor's cell. She heard the wailing of sirens, shouting voices and running feet.

Now is the time to escape, she thought.

She picked the lock of her door, and while the guards were rushing about in panic, she slipped out of the prison. She borrowed a police car which had been parked outside, and drove through the bright orange smog to the hills.

All the way home she had the siren turned on, the lights flashing, and she laughed her crazy laugh at the top of her voice.

Major Brassblow's bomb went off at midnight, exactly as he'd planned. First there was a small explosion, then the whole missile factory went sky-high with a lovely boom. He was standing at the window of his cell, and he saw the sky fill with fire. It was a moving sight.

In an instant, everyone in the prison was awake. Some cried out, 'World War Three!' Others yelled, 'The end of the world!'

The Major smiled to himself. What a pity that fiendish Doctor Foster couldn't see the end of her missile factory.

He would have happily stayed at the window, watching the fireworks, but an idea suddenly popped into his head. Now is the time to escape, it said. So the Major got out the tools he'd used to make the bomb, and he cut through the bars on the window. He climbed out into the prison yard.

He couldn't run very fast because the toes on each foot were twitching like a fly's legs. He didn't notice though. Someone had left a motorbike in the yard. It was most convenient. And because the guards were in confusion, they didn't hear or see the Major ride away.

The night was brightly lit, and the smog coloured flame yellow. The Major headed through it to the hills, singing a happy song to himself. He had one nasty moment when he thought he was being followed by a police car, but the car wooshed past him without slowing down. He got a dim image of a crazy driver with bushy hair.

Some time before dawn, he arrived at his house. He had to yell for the servants to unlock the gates. They came running in their dressing gowns.

'You're back from Washington, sir!' they cried, trying not to stare at his prison pyjamas and bare feet.

'Where's Jane?' he yelled. 'Send for Jane at once!'

'She's not here, sir,' they replied. 'She ran off and got married. To that Tim, sir. Doctor Foster's secretary.'

The Major's mouth opened. 'What?'

'She's been gone two weeks, sir.'

One of the servants blew his nose on a large white handkerchief. 'Terrible news about the factory, sir.'

'I wouldn't call it terrible,' said the Major. 'Now, Jane running away with that Tim fellow. That's terrible.'

The servant wiped his eyes. 'On the radio they said they thought a bomb had been planted. Enemy agents, they said.'

The Major stared at the servant. 'What? No, no. Carelessness, more like it. The place was never well run.' He yawned. 'I'm utterly exhausted, and I'm going to bed. No one is to wake me, you understand?'

'Yes, sir. Of course, sir.'

Major Brassblow marched on twitching feet into his bedroom. He pulled back the curtains, and looked down into the valley. The smog over Garpen Flat, glowed yellow and orange like a fire in a grate. The Major smiled sleepily. Who would have thought that the Foster Missile Factory could create so much colour and light?

He took off the prison pyjamas, put on his own of green and purple silk, then fell into bed and at once began to snore.

Doctor Foster woke up in her own comfortable bed in her own comfortable room. It was two o'clock in the afternoon. She was going to ring the bell for her secretary. Then she remembered that he'd gone. Treacherous Tim had run away and married the Major's secretary.

The Doctor scowled, but only for a moment. She remembered her brilliant bomb and her face lit up. She thought of the Major in his prison cell, and her face got brighter. If only she'd had the pleasure of telling him his tank factory had gone!

She rang her bell anyway, and a servant hurried in.

'Doctor Foster, Ma'am, I'm so glad you're awake. I said you were exhausted after your trip home from London, but they insist on seeing you.'

'They? Who's they?'

'Oh, everyone, Ma'am. The police, and the television and radio people, and the newspaper reporters, the photographers. Even the mayor of the town is here. It's about the factory, Ma'am.'

'Is that all!' Doctor Foster smiled and got out of bed. She put on a red satin dressing gown, covered in butterflies. 'I can't tell them anything about the factory. I've been away at a peace conference.'

The servant seemed nervous. 'Well, Ma'am, they keep asking if you're upset. I said, no, you weren't. I said you were taking it very well.'

The Doctor laughed. 'Of course I'm taking it well. How else would I take it?'

She had hardly spoken, when she saw herself in the mirror. She gave a small shriek of shock. Her hair was so frizzy, it stood up like a large bird's nest. She stared at the mirror, and thoughts rushed into her head. A cold feeling grew inside her.

'What factory?' she yelled at the servant.

The poor woman couldn't answer.

Doctor Foster opened the door to her balcony. 'No, no!' she shrieked. 'He wouldn't have! He couldn't have!' She rushed outside and looked over the edge, into the valley. The cold feeling grew as big as an iceberg. She knew exactly what had happened.

The smog had cleared. The town of Garpen Flat could be clearly seen, drab and bare, rows of brown brick houses on brown brick earth. At the south end of the town, lay the wreckage of the Tank Factory. To the north were the smoking ruins of her own precious Missile Factory.

Doctor Foster was so upset, she would have fainted if she had known how.

'Shall I tell the people downstairs you're awake, Ma'am?'

She didn't answer.

'What shall I say, Ma'am? They've been waiting since dawn.'

At that moment, the telephone beside the bed tinkled like a wind chime. The servant answered it, then said, 'It's for you, Ma'am.'

Doctor Foster came in from the balcony, like someone walking in her sleep. She sat on the bed and picked up the phone. 'Hello,' she said in a flat voice.

At the other end, another flat voice said, 'It's me.'

'Oh,' said the Doctor, and there was a long silence. For the first time ever they had no names to call each other.

The Major spoke in a choked-up voice, 'You know we're finished, don't you?'

'Done for,' she whispered.

'Up the spout,' he said.

'Down the drain,' she answered.

After another silence, the Major asked, 'Have you got people waiting to see you?'

'Yes.'

'Me too.'

'They think I've been at a peace conference in London.'

'They think I've been at disarmament talks in Washington.'

Then they both said together, 'What'll we tell them?'

The third silence was very long indeed. After it, Doctor Foster's voice had a little hope in it. 'If we get together,' she said, 'we could work something out. The important thing is, that we tell the same story.'

'Can we meet?' said the Major.

'We must meet,' she said. 'Where?'

'In my garden, under the fig tree. Sneak out. I'll be waiting for you.'

The Doctor's stomach felt slightly warmer. 'See you in five minutes,' she said.

Garpen Flat was full of rumours of war and H-bombs, enemies and spies, earthquakes and fires from heaven. No one had been killed by the explosions, but both factories were totally ruined, nothing left of them but smoking heaps of rubble.

When the people were sure that the town hadn't been invaded, they came out of their houses to look at the damage. They blinked red eyes in the sunlight, and saw an enemy worse than any invading army – unemployment.

'We've lost our jobs,' they whispered. 'Where will we work?'

A buzz of anxious questions could be heard from one end of the town to the other. What would happen to Garpen Flat? How would people live?

A woman heard a strange noise on her roof. She looked up and saw two pigeons cooing in the sunshine. She went inside and said to her husband, 'Oh well, it could have been worse. Suppose the factories had blown up during the day? We'd have all been killed.'

'I reckon it was enemy agents,' said her husband. 'Those two prisoners that escaped. They haven't been caught, have they? No, and I'll bet they're in another country by now. Enemy agents, that's what they'll be.'

That evening, all the news was cancelled for a special television announcement. People stopped whatever they were doing, to turn on their sets. Parents held their breath. Children hushed each other. Doctor Foster and Major Brassblow were giving a live broadcast from the television studio.

Major Brassblow was in his uniform, wearing all his medals. Doctor Foster wore her white laboratory coat and gold-rimmed spectacles which made her look very serious. They sat in tall, neat chairs beside the announcer. Behind them, on the wall, were the words *Garpen Flat Television.*

'Good evening, out there,' said the announcer. 'This has certainly been a day of days for Garpen Flat. What does it all mean? you ask. Who was responsible for the explosions? And where do we go from here? In the studio with the answers – the amazing, incredible answers – are Doctor Foster and Major Brassblow, just flown in from the other side of the world.'

The Doctor and the Major looked straight at the cameras. 'We are not going to waste words,' said the Doctor. 'The explosions were not caused by enemy agents. It was not sabotage. It was not terrorists, and no, it was not an accident. We will tell you now and without further ado – *we blew up our own factories*!'

All over Garpen Flat, air was sucked up in an enormous gasp.

Major Brassblow saluted the camera. 'Indeed, we did just that. At great personal loss and as an example to all nations, we have just destroyed the factories which made the best tanks and missiles in the world.'

Doctor Foster nodded. 'It is the solemn truth,' she said, then she stopped, surprised, for it was.

'Our consciences made us do it,' said the Major.

Doctor Foster coughed. 'You know that over all these years we have been dedicated to peace.'

'Absolutely dedicated,' said the Major.

'We have believed,' the Doctor went on, 'that the correct use of weapons could put an end to all wars. That's why we made weapons. That's why we sold them to far-off countries. We sold tanks. We sold missiles. Friends, we sold them because we thought they'd bring *peace*.' She took out her handkerchief and wiped behind her spectacles. 'I'm sorry to say that the rest of the world is not like Garpen Flat. Our enemies are everywhere, lying, cheating, turning all the good we do to evil. While the Major and I were away, we made an alarming discovery. The weapons we made were not being used to stop wars. They were being used to start them!'

'After the conference and the disarmament talks, we had a little meeting of our own. We decided that there was only one thing to do. We had to sacrifice everything!'

The Major nodded. 'That's what we decided,' he said, brushing the tears from his eyes. 'As soon as we got back to Garpen Flat, we – we had to destroy – blow up our fortunes – the work of a lifetime – our – our beautiful factories – ' He broke down completely and sobbed against his medals.

'Watch it, you fool!' hissed the Doctor. 'You're overdoing it.'

The Major gave a loud sniff. 'That is how we planned it.'

'With no loss of life, of course,' said the Doctor.

'No loss of life,' he said.

Doctor Foster smiled at the camera. 'But let us not consider our own loss, great though it is. Let us think of the people of Garpen Flat who will, right now, be worrying about their future. I say to all of you, we have already thought of your future. You will all have jobs. We'll plant trees and gardens for you. We'll build new peace factories to make furniture and clothing, factories for bread and buns, factories for sweets, factories for sun umbrellas. There will be plenty of work for everyone.'

'Absolutely everyone,' agreed the Major. 'Of course we'll only be able to pay you half wages for the – ' He stopped as the Doctor put her elbow in his side.

'This town will be the model for peace in the world,' she said, 'the most beautiful town in the country.' She got out of her chair and went to the back wall of the studio. 'Watch this,' she said to the camera. She reached for the letters that said Garpen Flat Television. She took down the 'p' from Garpen, turned it back to front and upside down, then replaced it. 'This town is now called Garden Flat!' she cried, raising her hands in the air.

'Garden Flat!' shouted the Major, jumping to his feet and saluting.

All over the town, air was breathed out in an enormous cheer.

Garden Flat, as it was now called, did become a model for peace in the world. The town soon had lawns and trees full of singing birds, and tomato and strawberry patches behind the houses. People lost their pallor. They had golden skins and bright eyes. Their children laughed and played in the clean air. And from every country in the world, came Queens and Princes, Presidents and Prime Ministers, to see the Major and the Doctor and the changes they had made.

Where the tank factory had been, Major Brassblow had put in a park and playground for children, with swings and slides and a ferris wheel. In the middle of the playground was his new liquorice allsorts factory with its sign 'Chew Liquorice for Peace.' Major Brassblow sold crates of liquorice allsorts to far-off countries. With this, and his other factories, he grew richer than ever.

On the old missile factory site, Doctor Foster had planted a beautiful garden where peacocks walked and fanned their tails. At one end of the garden she had a hat factory. She made flower hats and feather hats, clown hats, cowboy hats, policeman hats, judge hats, and paper hats for parties. Because she made a law that everyone had to wear a hat, the factory did very well.

Like many people who tell lots of lies, Doctor Foster and Major Brassblow began to believe their stories about the explosions. They even believed in their own goodness. They went from meeting to meeting in far-off countries, giving speeches about the great things they'd done for peace. They were very surprised and touched when they were awarded the World Peace Prize.

Statues of them were put up outside the Garden Flat Town Hall. When the statues were unveiled, the Doctor and the Major hugged each other.

'My good friend!' cried Doctor Foster, her voice full of emotion.

'Dear, kind Doctor!' the Major replied.